W9-BYM-325

Old Blue Buggy

by Fran Swift

illustrated by Carol Thompson

DUTTON CHILDREN'S BOOKS   NEW YORK

Text copyright © 2003 by Fran Swift
Illustrations copyright © 2003 by Carol Thompson
All rights reserved.

CIP Data is available.

Published in the United States 2003 by Dutton Children's Books,
a division of Penguin Putnam Books for Young Readers
345 Hudson Street, New York, New York 10014
www.penguinputnam.com

Designed by Richard Amari and Beth Herzog

Manufactured in China
First Edition
1 3 5 7 9 10 8 6 4 2
ISBN 0-525-45766-6

To Aimee, who loved Old Blue Buggy first
F.S.

To Jana
C.T.

When Henry was a tiny baby, his mother
found an old blue buggy at a yard sale.

Henry and his mom used Old Blue Buggy
every day. Henry lay on his back and looked
up at the trees or the clouds in the sky.
And as they went, Henry's mom would sing:

"Big buggy blue, blue buggy blue,
Be-bop-a, blue-bop-a, buggy-bop-a boo.

Bumpety-bump, clunkety-clunk,
Blue buggy, blue buggy, blue buggy blue."

Old Blue Buggy was big and rattly.
Henry laughed when it bounced along.
Sometimes his mom would
sit him up against his pillows.

Sometimes he closed his eyes
and had a nice nap.

Old Blue Buggy was big . . .

big enough to hold Henry and a friend.

Henry's mom could pile
lots of stuff into Old Blue Buggy.
There were always groceries to get . . .

clothes to take to the dry cleaners . . .

books to return to the library.

There were birthday parties to attend . . .

and daily outings in the park.

Old Blue Buggy was old and worn
around the edges. But Henry didn't mind.
As he grew, he loved to climb up
into Old Blue Buggy all by himself.

Sometimes he would
sit on his knees looking
straight ahead—
like the captain of a ship.

Sometimes he would
fly to the moon

or race across deserts.

Henry and his mom and Old Blue Buggy
were always on the go, and as they pushed
and bounced, they would sing:

"Big buggy blue, blue buggy blue,
Be-bop-a, blue-bop-a, buggy-bop-a boo.

Bumpety-bump, clunkety-clunk,
Blue buggy, blue buggy, blue buggy blue."

Henry grew older and bigger. He started
to use Old Blue Buggy less and less.

Henry wanted to walk,
or ride his trike, or push his wagon.

His mom would often do errands
while Henry was at preschool.

More and more,
they left Old Blue Buggy at home.

Henry's mom started to complain that
Old Blue Buggy was taking up precious
space in the foyer of their apartment.

She didn't like the way everything
seemed to get piled up in it—

like old newspapers

and bags of empty cans and bottles

and extra hats and sweaters.

Finally, during a big spring housecleaning,
Henry's mom decided Old Blue Buggy had to go.
Neither Henry nor his mom could think of who
might use worn-out Old Blue Buggy now.

Together, they bumped Old Blue Buggy into
the small elevator one last time.

They took it out to the sidewalk and left it
to be hauled off with the trash.
Then they sang, very softly and a little sadly:

"Big buggy blue, blue buggy blue,
Be-bop-a, blue-bop-a, buggy-bop-a boo.

Bumpety-bump, clunkety-clunk,
Blue buggy, blue buggy, blue buggy blue."

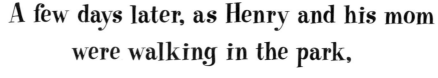

A few days later, as Henry and his mom
were walking in the park,

CLUNKETY BUMPETY

they heard a very familiar
clunkety-clunking sound behind them.
They turned and saw their Old Blue Buggy . . .

CLUNKETY CLUNK

being pushed by the lady everyone called
"Sara with all the bundles." She was smiling.
Old Blue Buggy was as full as ever. Only
this time it was full of Sara's many bundles.

Henry and his mom watched her go by,
and as they climbed up the hill
toward home, they couldn't help
humming happily to themselves:

"Big buggy blue, blue buggy blue,
Be-bop-a, blue-bop-a, buggy-bop-a boo.

Bumpety-bump, clunkety-clunk,
Blue buggy, blue buggy, blue buggy blue."